Sophia, Olivia, and Addison were excited to sp
Grandparents' house. Every year, they bake coo
for Santa on Christmas Eve. It is their favorite Christmas tradition.

Mom pulled into the driveway and Grandma was at the door to greet them. "Come on in girls, these Gingerbread cookies aren't going to bake themselves!" Grandma hollered.

They went into the kitchen to get started on the cookies. Like every year, Sophia cracks the eggs, Olivia melts the butter, Addison measures the flour while Grandma mixes it all together and puts the cookies in the oven to bake.

As the cookies baked, the girls went upstairs to play in their mom's old bedroom. While playing, Olivia noticed an old red box under the bed and pulled it out. The girls were curious and wondered what could be inside.

"Open it!" Addison said excitedly.

Olivia flipped the latch up and opened the box. Inside they found some old toys and a small red stocking, no bigger than their hand.

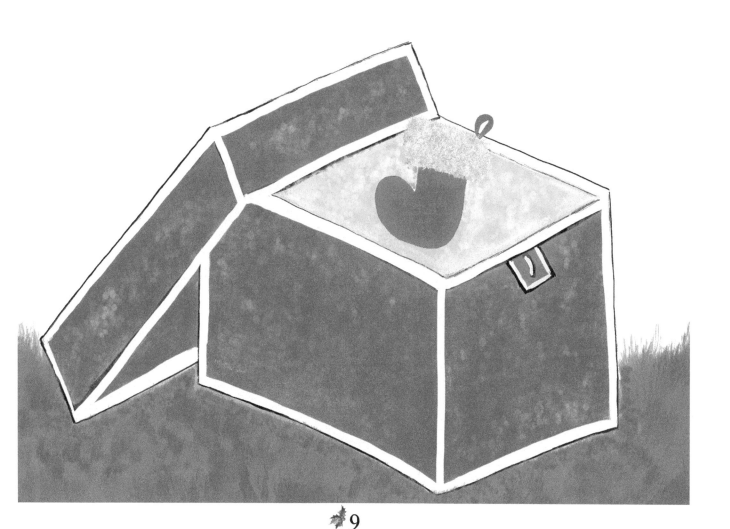

Addison pulled the little
stocking out of the box and
said, "Look, it's a tiny
Christmas stocking."

"Yeah, but it's way too small
to fit any presents. I wonder
what it's for?" Sophia asked.

"Let's go and ask Grandma!"
Olivia shouted.

The girls ran downstairs, to the kitchen, where Grandma was setting up the next batch of cookies. Olivia held the stocking up and asked, "What is this little stocking? We found it under Mommy's old bed."

Grandma and Grandpa looked at each other and smiled.

"It's **Santa's Magic Stocking** Mom used as a child." Grandma said.

"**Santa's Magic Stocking?** What's that?" Olivia asked

"Well, every Christmas, we would place this little stocking near the tree for Santa Claus. Then on Christmas Eve, Santa would leave presents inside." Grandma said remembering.

"How can anything fit in this little stocking?" Olivia asked. "Santa sprinkles magic dust on it to make it grow." Grandpa answered.

Addison was confused and asked, "It can grow?! How?" Grandpa explained, "The magic dust Santa sprinkles makes it grow to fit presents, then it shrinks again."

"I don't get it. How does it grow then shrink?" Olivia asked trying to stretch the little stocking herself.

"Santa's dust is magic!" Grandma said, sprinkling the little stocking with flour from her fingers.

"Our Christmas stockings have never shrunk. How come?" Sophia asked.

Grandma smiled and explained, "The stockings you have at home are already big. To see the magic, you must place a little stocking near the tree, instead of your big stocking."

"When Santa arrives, he will see the little stocking and sprinkle it with magic dust. The dust turns it into your big stocking. Then on Christmas morning, when you empty your big stocking and you are not looking, it shrinks. Like magic!" Grandma said.

"Will we see it shrink?"
Olivia asked.

Grandpa chuckled and said,
"You can try! But, in all my
years, I have not heard of
one child, anywhere, that
has seen it happen.

Let's go to get you girls
Santa's Magic Stockings to
hang this Christmas, so you
can see the magic for
yourself?"

"What a great idea!" Grandma agreed, "I know just the place to buy **Santa's Magic Stockings**. Grab your coats girls, we are going to the Christmas Store on the way home."

At home, the girls told Mom about the new magic stockings. "Oh yes, I loved my magic stocking!" Mom recalled. "It's my favorite memory of Christmas morning. I would wake up to find my little stocking was big and filled with candy and gifts. Then POOF!
Before I knew it, my stocking would be small again!"

Sophia turned to Mom and said, "Yeah, Grandma and Grandpa told us all about how it works! I cannot wait to see Santa's magic turn this little red stocking into my big stocking!

"Yes," Mom said smiling "It really is magical."

Later that night, the family decorated their freshly cut Christmas tree. It was a tall, beautiful pine tree that made the room smell like a forest! A trail of pine needles followed it in from the front door. Dad placed a sparkling gold star on the top of the tree. It was beautiful and the girls knew Santa would love it!

Mom found the perfect spot, over the fireplace, to hang their new magic stockings.

When they finished decorating, Addison began to wonder and asked, "Mom, can the stocking grow big enough to fit the bicycle I want for Christmas?" Mom giggled and said, "No sweetheart, they do not get that big. Just big enough for a few special gifts. You'll see now that you have one too."

Christmas morning finally arrived. Sophia, Olivia and Addison were bursting with excitement. They raced into Mom and Dad's room and jumped on the bed to wake-up them up. They had to know if Santa had come!

In the living room, toys were surrounding the tree and their stockings were big. Santa had come! Addison jumped up when she saw her new, big girl bike. It even had her name on it!

Olivia loved the new purple castle for her dolls. It was perfect! Sophia wrapped her arms around her new toy horse. It was the exact one she asked for in her letter to Santa.

The stockings were not little anymore! Now they were big and full of gifts! The girls hurried to empty the stockings to find all the wonderful things Santa left for them inside.

The girls kept looking at their big stockings to catch them to shrink. Sophia was playing with her horse when she turned to check again and found her stocking was small! "Look!" she shouted. "It shrunk! I can't believe it!" Sophia said giggling.

Looking for their big stockings, Olivia and Addison were surprised to see the little red stockings in their place.
"Ours shrunk too!" Addison said laughing.

The girls held their little stockings with wonder. The big stockings turned back into **Santa's Magic Stocking** just like Grandma said.
"WOW! Santa's magic dust really does work!" Olivia cheered.

The sisters just experienced the best kept secret of Christmas!
They promised to try and catch their stockings shrink next year
and a new Christmas tradition was formed.

The End

CPSIA information can be obtained
at www.ICGtesting.com
Printed in the USA
LVHW072010220921
698448LV00007B/146